Jesse Bo-T... Hard Work

I0622327

By;

Eddie J. Martin

A military deserter, a drug dealer, and pusher. A secret agent, a whoremonger, and a killer. Overall; just a regular guy.

Acknowledgement:

To my grandson: Jacob Richard Walker,

I finally got around to putting your favorite character in the mix; this one is for you.

C hapter one

Jesse was outside room 946 holding a young girl of say 20 years old and kissing her. He had his hands on her behind, and she had her arms around his neck and was giving him so much tongue. The tongue reached his tonsils, this was young girl, and he had to have her. They had just come back from a night on the town dinner, dancing etc. It was looking up to be a hell of a night. He took the key from her hand and commenced to open the apartment door. After he unlocked the door and opened it, she stepped through. She turned around and stopped him right there. He looked at her questioningly and said, "What's going on?" She told him she was sorry, but she did not do what he was thinking on the first date.

Jesse thought to himself that he had spent a good bit of money on this chick, and he would like something in return. Of course he said that to himself.

"Well, look," Jesse said, "What about me just coming in for a drink or two?"

"No," she said, "That will just lead to something else. How about a rain check?" she said, "Next time you won't be sorry."

Jesse was never a pushy guy, he was disappointed, but he could wait. As soon as she left, he walked down the hallway to the elevator. He called her a ***** under his breath. When he got to the lobby, he got on the phone and called another old girl that he knew that was just waiting for his call. He didn't have to wine and dine her. The only thing he had to do with her is stay up most of the night screwing and explaining where he had been for the last few days. He was up for the 1st, but he dreaded the 2nd.

****

He stopped by the McDonald's and purchased breakfast. He ordered sandwiches, egg, sausage, cheese, potato patties, 2 cups of coffee cream and sugar, and an extra sugar in one. He was ready to go a few minutes to 6:00 o'clock in the morning.

Gardenia was her name. She told Jesse that she was sorry, but she had to go to work. She had to be there because they were having a meeting. She thanked him for the breakfast. Jesse thought that his luck was hitting on nothing but bad. She asked him whether he would be there later that day at about 4:00 o'clock. Jesse felt as if he would die if he had to wait that long for a piece of tail. However, he said that he would be there if nothing came up to him. That was a code word for another girl. He was known for jumping out of one bed to another, and being back in time to jump back in the first before it was known he was gone. Those were the old days, he was a better man today. He would have one woman for a day or two, and find another the next day, that's practical.

He didn't wake up until one or two. When he got up, he washed up, got coffee and toast, and was ready to leave out the house when guess who walked through the door; Gardenia. He said, "I missed you babe. I was going to start looking for you if you didn't get here in the next 10 minutes."

"Jesse, you always talk that smack. I have good news and bad news for you."

"OK, tell me the good news."

"You can't get any, I'm on my period."

"That's the good news, do I want to hear the bad?"

"I have to go back to work right after I change cloths."

"What the hell!" Jesse said, "Where is the good news?"

"Is there ever going to be any time for Jesse?"

"Sure, there will Jesse. You just have to wait, and you always told me business came first, Right?" After gardenia was dressed and headed out the door, she asked him whether he would be in when she returned. However, she did not know when that would be.

"I will," Jesse said, "If nothing comes up."

****

Ten minutes after Gardenia left, Jesse was out the door. He reached in his back pocket and pulled out his little red notebook with all the essential information. Georgia, Livia, Dottie, and Claudia; I should stop there. He argued that there was no sense in getting too greedy.

He called Claudia, and a man answered the phone. Jesse asked for Claudia and the person said he was Claudia's husband. The respondent continued to ask him how he could help. Jesse told him he didn't think he could help him, and then he asked how long they had been married. The person said that they had been married for six months. Jesse remembered that was the last time he saw Claudia. She told him that if he left that time, she would not be there when he came back. I guess she was serious about that.

Next, he called Livia, and she told him straight up that she didn't want to see him again. She knew he was a player. She concluded that two players could not co-exist in a family. She said, "I will miss the sex; you are one in a million." She told him to lose her phone number.

Then there was Dottie, but her phone number had changed. The operator gave him her new number. He thanked her and asked whether she was she attached to anyone. She laughed at that, but he was not laughing, he was getting desperate. Anyone that knows him knows that he is a whoremonger. He knew that was a plus with some women, he just couldn't get enough, and they couldn't either. He thought about selling it, but he wouldn't feel right doing that, he would just give it away for free. Give it to the needy you might say, not the greedy.

"Hello?" Dottie said.

"Dottie, this is Jesse. How have you been babe? I have been thinking about you, and I have been trying to get back to you. However, it has not been easy."

"Jesse, I am ok. I was just thinking about you and wondering where you were. I was wondering whether I would ever see you again, and here you are. Are you coming over?"

"Are you at the same place?" Jesse asked.

"Same place Jesse, how soon can you get here?"

'I'm already there Dottie, you just don't see me."

He walked in the door, and there was Dottie fine as he remembered her, 5.5 and 120 pounds still looking good and well put together. He couldn't ask for anything more than that. The wait was worthwhile. There would not be a lot of talking here, you could bet on that. After the hugging, kissing, and disrobing, they finally made it to the bedroom, and then it was on. An hour later, laying up in bed, she brought him a drink, and then the questioning started. Where have you been? How long are you going to be here? Have you really been thinking about me? He lied all the way through. He was good at it, and besides, that is what he does. She got out of bed and walked to the bathroom. He watched her, she still had that fine behind that rolled with each step she took. She stopped and looked back at him and said, "What?" He said, "Jesse, you are one lucky mother jumper."

******

C hapter 2
Luna walked into Diego's office and humbled himself. "Tell me about it Luna, tell me how such amount of drugs could get away from you? Is it because you didn't have enough security? I thought it was sufficient. So, tell me what happened?"

"The only thing I could figure out Mr. Diego is that we have an undercover in our mix. We hired several people a while back, and I think one of them is a spy. They knew where the stash was, and we couldn't help that since our other men had been arrested. We had no choice but to show them."

"We had about 1000 pounds of marijuana, and we had the cocaine bricks in a different location, how was it that they hit both locations? We can't have this Luna. We have to make up for what we lost. However, the crucial thing is finding the guy that snitched on us. What do you suggest?"

"We have to set him up," said Luna, "That is the only way I think we will catch him. But then, we have to put more drugs out there to convince him it is worth snitching for. Do you think you will be able to persuade the cartel to trust us with another stash?"

"I'm sure I can, but they are not too keen on trust. When I tell them what happened, they may go along with me since I have been with them for long, but even friendship will go down the tube because of money. Get the people out to try to find out who this undercover guy is, and don't use the ones that recently came in the organization.

Luna left Diego's office and picked up Basil from the front. They went to a small club, and Luna told Basil they needed to come up with something. He had a feeling that Diego would eventually look at him as far as ripping off the drugs. "I know I have been with him a long time, but his mind is not there. We need to find out whoever is snitching on us, and to find out quick. Can you come up with anything?"

"Not right off Luna, no more than what you have, but I have heard of an old buddy of mine that is back in town. He is one smart sucker, and if anybody were to find this guy, it would be him."

"What is his name basil?"

"Bo-T; that's his name, Jesse Bo-T."

"Why haven't I ever heard of him?"

"Well, he doesn't stay here in Columbia, he's in and out. He deserted from the military when he was in Germany over some drugs, and from what I hear, he has been all over the world. They haven't caught up with him yet."

"How well do you know this Bo-T? Is he dependable? Does he know how to follow orders?"

"He is the best Luna, take my word on it. He was in the military."

"Would you be able to get in touch with him?"

"That shouldn't be a problem. I just heard he is back in town. A little looking and word of mouth shouldn't be any problem. He is a ladies' man, so, the first place I would go looking is the ladies."

"Find and bring him Basil. Let me talk to him and I will know whether he is right for what we need.

******

C hapter 3

A few days later, Basil and Jesse walked into an unknown location and they met Luna. Basil introduced Jesse to Luna who offered Jessie a drink. One thing led to another, and Luna wanted to know all about Jesse and where his travels had taken him since he left the military. Jesse brought him up to date, leaving Dorothy and Janice out of the conversation.

"Has Basil told you the kind of job we do?" Luna asked.

"I can guess," Jesse said. He was always in the drug business.

"Did he tell you about the snitch in the organization, and we need to route him out?"

"No,' Jesse said, "He never told me all that."

"We need to find out who this person is and get him out. We are losing too much money by him being around. Do you understand?"

Jesse nodded his head in the affirmative.

"We need you to go undercover, and find out who this person is. Can you do that?"

"If the money is right," Jesse said, "I could do that."

"I'm sure you will have no problem with the money. If you want a job after this job is done, it is there for you, how's that?"

'It sounds good to me," Jesse said.

"We will introduce you to the rest of the people, and then we will leave everything up to you. Do what you have to do to rectify things, although we would like to know our snitch.

****

A few days later, at a new undisclosed location, Jesse met up with the other crew.

First, there was Joel, he was known to be good with any size boat.

Then there was Levi, Levi was supposed to be good ripping off automobiles and getting them salvaged. The third member was Simon. Simon was good at knifing people; some say he was the best. The fourth was Eli. He was the crew's drug man that could tell you anything about drugs. By smell alone, he could tell where the drugs came from.

One of these guys was the insider for the police, but by looking at them, Jesse couldn't tell which one. All looked shady, and they would cut your throat for a nickel. But Jesse learned that this job was something different, pick-up and delivery. They were two dangerous jobs, and that is how the crew got screwed. One of these guys turned the others in, and two ended up getting killed. So, the replacement was three men including Jesse.

Basil told Jesse he thought that the feds wanted the big boss, and that would be Diego. That was the reason they had not busted the whole crew. Once they get close enough, they would hit everybody. The only one who knew who he was is Luna, and it was hard to get anything out of him.

"Have you ever seen him Basil?"

"I have never seen him, and I don't want to see him. The last ones that did see him went over the cliff. I don't care who he is or what he looks like, I just want to be paid."

For the next few weeks, Jesse and the crew picked up and delivered the drugs from one location to another. It was really hard work. Jesse wasn't used to anything like that. He usually sat back and let the workers do it all, and he would supervise.

Every job has a break, and the crew had one too. They went to the village to pop a few drinks and whatever they could get their hands on. Jesse was looking for the little Mamas, which was the first thing. He took a large bottle in the bedroom with him and commenced to get into both. It was not long before there was a knock on his door. Basil told him that they had to go, something important had come up. He was lucky because ten minutes before that, he wouldn't have gotten up, and that's for true.

Basil told him that the feds were headed to their last pick-up place. He wanted to get there to collect any material they had left.

"How did they get on to this place so quick?' Jesse asked.

"It is our snitch, he is dead good on the job, but we will get him. How are you doing about locating him?"

"I'm on the job Basil, give me time."

"You already have three weeks now, how many more do you need?"

"Jesse didn't give Basil a reply. He had been on the job, but he couldn't follow everyone at a time."

Joel was the first one. One night after making a delivery, he followed him to a small apartment. He met up with some little Mama, and they stayed in all night. When he looked through the window, they were getting at it hard and heavy. After days of following him, Jesse felt that there were no moves. He was convinced that Joel was not with the feds. Therefore, he got off him and went to the next guy, Levi.

Levi had his little secrets too. After the drop offs, he went to an off-the-wall hole. At the wall, he met up with some guy, they went to an apartment, and he followed them. He got a chance to look in on them. He didn't want to say what he saw, but damn, Levi fooled him. He didn't stay there that much longer, he was a ladies' man.

Simon was something different. All he did was stay around the cabin and play crossword puzzles. He stayed with him for a few days to see if he made any types of calls to anyone he would be suspicious of. However, he did none of that, he just sat there dreamy-eyed. He did not talk much. Jesse tried to get what he could out of him, but all he had to say was a 'uh-huh,' and 'ha-ha'; he was weird.

When they got back to work, he had one more guy to survey, and then he would have to start back over again. If it was not him, that should be fun.

Basil had found another stash house and told him no one knew about this place except him. He told him that they were to keep it a secret. Jesse did not tell him that there was only one guy he had to survey, and if it weren't him, then he would have to go back to the old drawing board.

They worked till two that morning, and he kept his eye on Eli, but there was nothing. He jumped in his bunk like the rest of the crew. The following night, they finished up and went to bed. Twenty minutes later, he got up and left the building, and Jesse was right behind him. Half a block away was a phone booth with the light out. From his vantage point, he saw Eli make a call and stayed on the phone for ten minutes before hanging up. He left his spot and made it back to the shack, and into bed. Five minutes later, Eli eased the door open and got into bed. Well, Jesse said to himself, it looks like I have found my man.

The following night, he met at a different location, and to his surprise, it was a woman. She was dressed in old street clothes and she was pushing a grocery cart. He went into the alley with her, and they talked for a good ten minutes before he left and went back to the shack. Jesse knew where he was going, so, he followed the woman. Not far away, an official-looking automobile picked her up and he couldn't follow any further. He thought then he didn't have to look any further. All he had to do was to find out what Luna wanted to do with him. He had a feeling that he knew, but that would be extra.

****

C hapter 4

The following day, Jesse met Basil at the cantina. He informed him what he found out about Eli, and who he met. There was no doubt it had to be the law. He then asked him what he wanted to do.

"I have to talk to Luna first, and I guess he will talk to Diego. However, I will let you know soon. We are on a lag right now, so we have time no matter what we do."

A day later, Basil got back to Jesse and told him that he spoke to Luna. Luna had in turn spoken to Diego, and they both wanted him gone; they wanted him to do it. Basil asked whether Jesse had any problem.

"No," Jesse said, "If the money is good."

"The money will be good Jesse, just take care of that job. Don't take long since we are about to move another shipment soon. We found another stash house with a bad batch of weed. It is something that we can afford to lose. We are getting the word out that we will be moving the stuff in a day or two. That is enough time to give him time to make his contact. Will that work for you?"

"I will pick my own time and place," Jesse said, "Don't worry about me, just do what you have to do and move on."

Two nights later, after being told about the stash house and when they were moving the product, at 3:00 o'clock that morning, Eli left the shack and went to the phone booth. While in the phone booth, Jesse walked up to the door and tapped on it with his .38 with silencer. Eli turned around, saw Jesse, and his eyes turned the size of sausages especially after he saw the gun. He was still talking, then he dropped the phone. Jesse made sure he saw the weapon pointing at him. He shot him through one of his eyes and then shot him again in his head, and left the scene. There would be no rendezvous that night.

The cops came the next afternoon and picked up the body. There was no concern about a body in that neighborhood since it was known for killings. The only difference was that the person that was killed was an informer, one of theirs.

By that time, the crew had left and they were even wondering, who killed Eli?

The only thing anyone could come up with is that Eli had gotten himself into something that no one knew about. Too bad, they said he was a good guy.

Basil was happy, Luna was happy, and Mr. Diego was also happy. They paid Jesse, and he was happy, overall, it was a moment of happiness. Jesse got a raise and was introduced to Mr. Diego. They said there was grandiose things in the making for him.

The street person with the shopping cart was in the area, and she called her superior's. She told them what had happened, and they would have to get another inside person. They told her not to worry since they had someone.

"Can you tell me about it?" She asked.

"In time agent, in time."

C hapter 5

Jesse spent some time at Dottie's. There was a lot of love making, dinner, dancing, and going back home. There was intense love making every time he was with her. He thought that merry-making was all they had in common, but then there was nothing wrong with that. She asked him a lot of questions about where he had been and what he had been doing? Questions! Questions! Questions! He knew he would get that once he saw her again. He would have to make the periods between visits longer, if he could hold out that long. She said some guy had been around looking for him, but she didn't know what to tell him or where he was. Weeks later, the same guy came over again and asked the same question, and she gave him the same answer. He asked her whether he was from there and how often he came around. She didn't lie, she told him what she knew. She told him that Jesse would leave and come back maybe six months to a year later. He told the stranger that Jesse was a traveling man and never stayed in one place for too long. If he left his address and phone number, she would make sure he received it, but he never did.

"What did he look like?" Jesse asked.

"He was about your height with a baseball cap on his head, and wore blue jeans and Plaid shirt. He looked like he was wearing brogans. He was about 170 pounds, he had some shady looking eyes, and a heavy mustache. He really looked like a dead fish to me."

"What type of car was he driving?" Jesse asked.

"He had no car Jesse, he was walking. I noticed him getting on a bike further down the street, and he took off headed that way."

"Do you know him?" She asked.

"I don't think so, but I suspect he will be back. Maybe he is one of those old boys I knew in the military and he wants to hit me up for a loan. I will be here for a few days, and we figure it out."

On the third day, a knock came at the door, and Jesse answered. It was the fish.

"Jesse Bo-T?" He asked, "Can we talk?"

"Sure, we can talk." Jesse walked out of the door and closed it behind him. "There is a small club about a block from here, we can go there."

"Do you have a name?" Jesse asked.

"Jamal," the Fish said.

"How did you happen to find me?" Jesse asked.

"A friend of a friend," Fish said.

Until they got into the club, none said anything more until they set down and ordered drinks.

Jesse looked the Fish over, and he appeared shabby. There was no need to walk around town looking like that, but hey, what the hell did he know? People can fool you.

After the drinks came, the fish set back in his booth, looked at Jesse and told him, "Did you know that there was a hit out on you?"

Jesse looked at the Fish and told him, that he was not aware. The Fish said, "Well, there is, and there is quite a bit of money on your head."

"Were you planning on collecting it?" Jesse asked.

"I was asked to take the contract," the Fish said.

"And what did you decide?" Jesse asked.

"I'm still thinking about it," the Fish answered.

"I thought that maybe if I talk to you, you would offer more money than the people that offered the contract."

"Who are these people?" Jesse asked, "Is it anybody I know? I guess I would have to know them if they want me dead, right?"

"You might say that," the Fish said, "But then, if the money is right and we can come to an agreement, I would tell you that too"

"Let's say I go along with your proposition, then what?"

"You pay me the money I ask for, and I tell you who put the hit on you. Then, I would go away; it is as simple as that."

"How much are we talking about?" Jesse asked.

"$10,000 cash, American," the Fish said.

"That is a lot of money."

"I was offered less, but I figured due to the circumstances, you wouldn't mind paying me more," the Fish replied.

"How long do I have to think about it?"

"Not long," the Fish said, "I have wasted a couple of weeks on you already."

"How about 48 hours (about 2 days), and even if I did agree to your proposition, I would need time to get the money."

"I don't know if I believe that Mr. Bo-T, I hear you always have a way of getting your hands on extra money. However, 48 hours is ok. I'll have to tell you Mr. Bo-T, there is no reprieve."

"When do I get the name of your employer?"

"Right after you pay me the money," Fish said.

"Tell me something," Jesse asked, "If I were to let you in my house, would you have killed me right there?"

"Yes, I would have Mr. Bo-T. But then, I would have had to kill the girl too; it is just business. I hope that you understand. She seems to be a nice girl."

"How do I contact you?' Jesse asked.

The Fish brought out a pen and wrote down a number. "You can contact me right there, and when you call, make sure it is around

10 or 11 P.M."

Two days later, at 10:30 P.M, Jesse contacted the Fish and told him that he had decided to pay him. The Fish asked him whether he had the money, and Jesse told him that he did. He asked the Fish to set up a meeting. The Fish told him to go to an elementary school on the other side of town. Jesse asked him why he had chosen a distant location, and the Fish told him that he didn't want any hiccups along the way. At 1:00: AM, he met the Fish. Jesse had the cash in a canvas bag. The money was in small denomination and $10,000 like he had promised. They met in a stairway, and Jesse handed him the money in the bag. The Fish opened the bag and his eyes got big. He started counting the money, but he took his eyes off Jesse. Jesse pulled out the .38 with the silencer on it. When the Fish looked up and saw the gun, he dropped the money. "Wait a minute," he said, "Just you wait a minute. You gave me your word, but I see you are not going to honor it."

"There is no honor among thieves, now you know that."

"Who sent you?" Jesse asked, "Who put the hit on me?"

"I can't tell you that, you'll kill me if I do, I'll have nothing to bargain with."

Jesse promised not to kill him if he told him what he wanted to know. "Do you promise?" The Fish asked.

"Who sent you?" Jesse asked again, "Who put the hit on me?" Then, Jesse pulled back the hammer on the .38. The weapon looked like a bazooka pointing at Fish, and he began to talk, and talk. He told it all hoping that Jesse wouldn't kill him. Right after Jesse got all the information he thought he could get from the fish, he said, "Remember when I told you I wouldn't kill you if you told me the truth? Well, I lied. You didn't really think I was going to give you all this money, did you? What a fool!" As Fish put up both his hands and was about to speak, water started running down his pants; he had urinated. Jesse shot him through the mouth and then through the back of the head.

JESSE BO - T...HARD WORK

****

C hapter 6

She walked down the six-floor hallway to room 623. She wore high-heel shoes, a long dress that touched the ankles, a scarf around her head, short golden earrings, had a long nose, and enlarged kissable lips. She had a long neck like a model and a long body like a mermaid. When she reached room 623, she just walked in and did not knock. In the room was a secretary behind a large desk who addressed her as Rosetta. She told her to go right in as he was expecting her.

Agent Reebok was sitting behind a larger desk than the secretary's. He stared first before addressing her. He said, "For a minute there Rosetta, I didn't recognize you. The last time I saw you, you looked like a bag woman especially when you were pushing that cart; now you look like a movie star. I must say you sure know how to change your appearance."

"Well, I guess that's good then, right?" Rosetta replied. "I think my assignment is over since Eli was murdered. Do you know who killed him?"

"It was one of the men in the crew, we are sure of it. They must have found out who he was and got rid of him. It will be your job to find out who did it. This assignment isn't over yet, we are still after the people pushing drugs and their boss. The group has moved from one location to another, and we are having a hard time catching up with them. Diego, who we thought was the boss is not; there are others above him. We plan to get the bird in hand, and let the others fall where they may."

"So, are you telling me that the street person is no more?" Rosetta asked.

"That is about it, but there is something else that we know you'll be good at. If you recall, there were three to four men hired with the crew. One of the men that you knew as Eli was our undercover person, but we had another undercover person backing him up. He stayed out of view, but he was there, he is still there.

Out of the three new men, there is one that we think you could get close to and work your way into the club. His name is Jesse Bo-T, and he is known as a woman's man. He loves women, and does not seem to get enough of them. We think you are the one to get close to him. He has moved up into the organization, but that is even better."

"Do you want me to contact this under cover person, and how do I do it?"

"Our other undercover agent is named Simon. He will contact you through crossword puzzles. He will find a way to give you the puzzle he has been working on, and you will pass it on to us, simple."

"You say he plays crossword puzzles, what! Is he a geek?"

"Maybe, but he is an awful smart geek enough to be fooling them."

"So, where do I locate this Jesse Bo -T?"

****

Meanwhile, Jesse made it back from Dottie's place. He was talking to Mr. Diego and he told him that they had problems.

"Right after you left, we got hit again. Luckily for us, our men got out of there just in time with the stash intact. But what is puzzling is that they still knew where we were at. We have an informer, another informer in our midst. We can't seem to get away from them."

"Well, if there is another one that we missed, then we will have to take care of him too. It is just a matter of time, and we must roll our shipment."

"Well Jesse," said Diego, "You took care of the last informer, I'm sure you will take care of this one. I hope this will end it."

"Let me work on it Mr. Diego," said Jesse, "We will find him."

Days later, at one of the local clubs, Jessie and Luna were having a drink. Luna pointed out a girl that they hadn't seen before, and naturally, Jesse was interested.

"Luna, let me have this one, she surely looks good enough to me." Jesse walked over to the young lady who was wearing a low cut off the shoulder black dress and asked if he could buy her a drink. Rosetta looked him over and said why not, and it started from there. They stayed in the club till closing, and Jesse took her home. He stayed with her for two days. It looked like she was the one. He thought to himself that he would stay with her till the end of time, but then, he knew he was lying. The idea sounded good.

Back at the rendezvous point, Luna asked him whether he was trying to make a home.

"Well, nothing like that," Jesse said, "When you find something good, you try to hold onto it and not let anyone else move in."

There was a night when Rosetta and Jesse were in the club having dinner, and Simon happened to walk in. Jesse introduced him to Rosetta. They spoke like they didn't know each other, and seemed to get along very well except when Jesse went to the bathroom. Simon passed Rosetta a crossword puzzle that was in the local paper, and when Jesse appeared, he happened to see this. Rosetta told him, "I didn't know your friend was into crossword puzzles, I dabble in those myself."

"Well, you got me there," Jesse said, 'I know nothing about cross-word puzzles. They look boring to me, but since I met Simon, that is all he does when he is not working."

"Working?" Rosetta said, "You never said what type of job you do."

It was Simon who got on another subject and acted like he never heard her. Jesse said nothing.

Rosetta and Jesse left the club, but not before she picked up the newspaper that had the crossword puzzle in it.

Jesse is not an especially smart man, but he is not dumb either. It took a few more incidents with the newspaper, which he caught on, and passed on to Basil his thoughts. They decided to set a situation so that when Simon passed on the crossword puzzle to Rosetta, they would have someone follow her and see where she goes with it. If it were to the authorities, then they had their people.

It happened the way they thought it would. Jesse and Rosetta went to dinner. As usual, Simon came up with the newspaper and gave it to Rosetta. After dinner, Jesse took Rosetta back home and on the pretense of things he had to do, he left her there.

An hour later, a car pulled up to Rosetta's home. A person got out, went to her door, she passed on the newspaper to him, and he left. Levi was watching all this from an alley across the street.

****

C hapter 7

Everyone was there; Joel, Levi, Simon, Luna, and Basil at the new location to pick up the stash. This location was far out into the woods with only a dirt road to get there. They had the regular two-and-a-half-ton truck and a 4-wheel van.

They walked into the building and found that there was nothing there. Then, everyone turned around and looked at Simon. Two of the men grabbed him and shook him down. They found the little automatic on his ankle, a whittling knife, and also took the pen he used for the crossword puzzle from him. They set him in a straight back chair and tied him to it. Simon didn't have to ask what it was all about. He knew what was going on, but they questioned him anyway.

Simon wasn't a very tough guy, but he was smart. He knew if he didn't tell them what they wanted to know, it would go bad for him. This way, at least, he would get a quick death.

Simon was smart, he told them everything they wanted to know, and more. He told them who Rosetta was, and the part she played.

Just like Simon had predicted, they didn't torture him much. One quick shot in the head, and it was over. Disposing off the body was not hard because they were in the Woods.

A few nights later, Jesse picked Rosetta up for dinner. As they were eating, she made reference to Simon not showing up, and she wondered what had happened to him.

"He probably picked up something for himself," Jesse said, "I told you he is unpredictable." After they danced and had more drinks, they went to her home, went to bed, and had sex. The next morning, she fixed Jesse breakfast comprising of toast and coffee. She asked Jesse to stay for the night, that is, if he had nothing to do. He said, "Sure, why not? But I will be thinking about you until I return." Before he left, he told her that he loved her, and he would miss her. At 11:00 AM, he departed.

At 2:00 PM that afternoon, she was dressed and was headed down to her boss's office. She thought about Jesse and how she liked him. It had happened before, a secret agent falling for a person of interest. What he said to her before he left was sweet; that he would miss her, and that he loved her.

 As she was crossing the street in front of the federal building, she never noticed a large semi-tractor trailer bowing down on her. It hit her, knocking her a good 50 –feet and killing her instantly.

*****

Two weeks later Jesse was at Gardenia's home. She seemed surprised to see him. "It's me babe, did you miss me?"

"Well, it has been some weeks now," Gardenia said, "where did you disappear to? I was hoping you would be back way before now. I even sent people out to look for you." She told Jesse to sit down, and she sat down across from him and spoke. "I really don't appreciate you doing what you did to me. I came back to the house looking for you hoping to have some great sex, but there was no Jesse. I don't like that, and I don't like what you did to me."

And then Jesse said, "Is that why you put a hit out on me? Sent the fish after me? Why did you have to do that?"

'You will never do that to me again Jesse, and I hate you for it. I really hate you for it. My expectations were high.'

"Will you do that again gardenia? I would hate you doing that to me and looking over my shoulders all the time."

"I may and I may not, it all depends on how I feel. You didn't have to bring that box of candy with you to make amends. I told you the way I feel. Take that box of candy and get your ass out of here."

"First, let me do this," Jesse said. He untied the ribbon and opened the box. He brought out a .38 pistol, and beside it was a silencer. He screwed it on securely. She looked at the weapon, looked at Jesse, and her eyes got large as a German two-cent piece. After Jesse screwed on the silencer, he pointed it at her and told her, "You know little about me, because if you did, you would know I can't go around with a threat like that over my head. I must do something about it. You told me your plans, and, in my job, I can't have that."

Gardenia started to explain and cry, but Jesse would have none of it. "Don't cry Gardenia, don't cry. It is all for the best.

You have had your chance, and you must admit I gave it to you, but you acted disrespectful. So, Miss Gardenia, I'm going to do what I must do. However, this is going to hurt me more than you." After the brief confession, he shot her between the eyes. She laid back in the chair and you couldn't tell whether she was sleeping or dead. It did not matter; he was out of there.

****

C hapter 8

A while later, after things seemed to be going well Lune talked to Jesse and said, "You know, I think it is time for Mr. Diego to find another job. He has been in this one for too long, and I no longer trust him. I think I could do a better job, what do you think?"

"Well, if anyone was to take over," Jesse said, "It would be you. So, what are you trying to say?"

"I have already said it Jesse, Mr. Diego must go, and I'm taking over. The question is, are you with me?"

"You know I recently got a promotion, how is that going to affect the plan?"

"You won't have to worry about that at all Jesse, you may even get another promotion on top of that one."

"What about the other men, will they go along with this?"

"They will go along with whatever we say, they follow orders Jess. We will look for a paycheck which will make it right for them."

"And what about Mr. Diego's boss, he has a boss you know?"

"What do you know about them?" Luna asked.

"I know he has one," Jesse said, "Just like you said, he is not that smart to be running this whole operation on his own. They may not like it very much if you do what you are planning to do."

"It won't matter to them if the operation is running smoothly and they are getting their cut. We may offer them a little incentive to make them happy."

"I need to think on this, when do you want my answer?"

****

At the federal building, 9th floor, room 923, agent Reebok and his section sat around a conference table. "We have lost at least three of our people. One was a hit and run that may be associated with the assignment she was on; we should have closed that case down long ago if it wasn't for wanting the kingpin. Now we have lost three people. Rosetta, I liked Rosetta, and she was one of us. We must retaliate, if not for us, then for her. Now this is an order, we are going after those people like never before. We don't have to go by the book to do it."

"Are you telling us it is open season on the crew?" One asked.

"That is what I'm saying. We know about everyone in the crew, so, if we must eliminate them one at a time, that is what we will do. However, make it look accidental if you can. You have your assignments, get it done."

"Sir," one of the groups asked, "Are we going to replace Rosetta?"

"No, we are going out for the kill, this is ours to do."

****

The first one was Joel, he liked to go fishing when he was not working for Mr. Diego. He would spend hours on the Bank of the River, fishing and drinking. That is where they got next to him. They came in a boat and pretended they had trouble. They shot him in the head and tossed the body in the boat. They took him out to the deepest part, weighed him down, and threw him overboard.

Next was Levi. They knew that he loved riding horses. They caught him riding in a ranch at the countryside. They made the horse veer up and throw him off. He laid there on the ground unconscious.

There was a wild stallion in one of the corrals that had not yet been broken in. They put him in the stall with him, and he did the rest.

Meanwhile, Jesse was having a drink with Mr. Diego and getting a feel on when to blow him away. He had been thinking about his situation, and weather going with Luna would be a better option compared to going with Diego. He would prioritize his situation above others. So, he decided to tell Diego the proposition that Luna had made to him; he was to eliminate Diego.

After astonishing disbelief, Diego asked Jesse whether he was sure of what he had said. Jesse replied with the affirmative, and asked Diego what he wanted to do about it.

"I felt that soon he would want to be the boss," Diego said, "But I didn't think it would be this soon. So, Jesse, in that case Mr. Luna is no longer needed in this crew. Would you mind taking care of him for me?"

"Is that what you want to do?" He asked Diego, "He may still be of some use down the road."

"No Jesse, it is like this, if I don't do him first, he will just get somebody else to do me, and where would that leave me? I'll tell you, dead. When can you do it?" Diego said, "I think you should do it as soon as possible."

Meanwhile, at the stash house, Basil was telling Luna about their two men, Joel and Levi. "We can't find Joel, and Levi was found dead at a horse ranch."

"Is it coincidental? I don't think so. I think someone is killing up our men. Who do you think it could be? It could be another group trying to move in on us."

"I don't know Basil, but I'll run it across Diego and see if he knows anything. Speak to Bo-T, and see if he heard anything. It looks like we require more men. We have a shipment due in two nights, and we must tackle that.

*****

The pickup night went smoothly. They picked up the shipment from the stash house and took it to another stash house. Another group would pick it up and take it from there. Everything went fine until...

Basil was driving down to his girl's house as usual after a drop off. He noticed a dark colored vehicle behind him. He didn't go straight to his girl's house, but drove around town trying to figure out whether it was the feds or another group that he didn't know of. They started closing in on him, and he pressed the gas for more speed. As he sped up, they brought in more speed, and it looked like they were overtaking him. He tried all the tricks he knew on evasion, but none worked. He reached in the glove compartment and brought out a .45 and made sure that it was loaded. A little further down the road, they ran into him. They pushed him off the road, and at that speed, the car flipped. Luckily, he was only bruised and could make it out of the car. By that time, the other car had stopped, and two men were coming back towards him. He didn't know who they were, but he knew they meant him no good. He started firing; he fired the entire clip in the gun hitting both men, and then he started running as fast as he could to the nearest phone booth to call Luna. They needed to stop this, regardless of who the men were.

****

C hapter 9

Reebok entered the hospital room at St. Elizabeth Hospital, and his men were laid up in bed side by side. Both would live, but they would be out of action for the next six months. One had a leg wound and the other was shot in the foot. Reebok was elated that the men were ok, but he was also mad as hell that they came up short on getting the third in command of the crew. Nevertheless, he knew it would be soon, and the sooner the better.

One of his men came up with setting Bo -T up again, but Reebok didn't think that would work a second time. He said, "It is better to go after them the way we have. Wherever we find them, we will take them out and the hell with the law." He swore to put his people on the street, and keep them on the street day and night until he found them.

Meanwhile, Jesse had got together with Basil and Luna with Mr. Diego. He decided to put off the hit on Luna until all this was over. He wondered who was killing his people. It was not the cops because they are for law and order, so it wouldn't be them. Mr. Diego suggested that everyone lay low until they found out who was doing all the killing. "I wouldn't even go out to the clubs if I were you," he said, "Better yet, maybe we should take a little vacation. Everyone should go their separate ways, and we will meet back here whenever."

"What about the people who receive the drugs?" Basil said, "What are we going to tell them?"

"We will have to work something out with them because it is too hot to move now," Mr. Diego said. "They know what we are going through. Don't think that they do not, they are just waiting around to see what we are going to do about it. Once they find out we cannot control our own organization, then they will find a new distributor."

"Well, it is not the cops, I would bet my life on that," Basil said, "These guys that were after me wanted to kill me, and I felt that I just got the upper hand."

"I don't know," said Jesse, "It could be the cops. I wouldn't be surprised if it was not, we put down three of their people. They are just like anyone else. When you attack them, it is kill or be killed, and it looks like it right now. They are doing all the killings."

"I'll tell you what," Luna said, "We have people on the street that can find out who these guys are, and in some instances, get them to do us a favor. We must know who they are."

"I sure don't like the idea of running and hiding," said Jesse, "But I guess until we find out who they are, that is what we will have to do."

****

Reebok's people including their informers were all over town. They searched the Barber shops, liquor stores, and every place that they thought the crew had gone. At one time or another they passed around and went to the shady parts of town, then the effluent parts of town, just in case, nothing. While they were out looking for the crew, the crew was also looking for them. Just like you would imagine, they eventually met one another, and word went out. Like on a battlefield, each knew where the enemy was, who they were, and where they were.

The first thing Diego did was move his headquarters and hire more people of different nationalities. He also added a couple of women in the mix. It was a real eye opener to find out that the police were killing his people, and he kept saying to himself, "No, this just isn't the way it is done. The cops are the good guys, and it is the bad guys we kill, only when we have to, only guys like us. It could be times when we have to kill others that try to take ours and incarcerate us while doing so, that is fair! But, these guys are cheating their killing with a badge, and that is damn right dirty. This killing cannot be authorized. I have a feeling that these are some rogue cops just trying to get back at us."

"Should we start retaliating on them?" Basil asked, "They brought it on themselves."

"I don't think we should start doing that," said Jesse, "Then we will really have them on our *ass*. We should wait awhile, and it will die down especially after we put two of them in the hospital. What about this?" Jesse said, "If we get into a pinch and must put them down, then that is just what we will do. They will get nothing for free here."

"That's it then," Diego said, "Gentlemen, it is business as usual. There is a shipment due tomorrow night, I expect everyone will be there."

This load was the largest they ever attempted to ship. There were two large two and a half-ton trucks, one van, and 10 men. The old barn where the drugs were stored was almost full, and they started right off loading the trucks. Basil was overseeing the loading and Luna was overseeing Basil.

Overall, the loading went well. Once loaded, they started out the van in the lead. Five miles down from the barn, all hell broke loose on them. One police vehicle blocked the road and another came up the rear and blocked the back. On the sides from the bush, men pounced on them. Basil did not go too easily it took more than fourteen rounds to kill him. The other men tried to surrender, but the police acted as though they did not hear anyone. Luna found out that he was surrounded and would be taken, but they continued firing at him and there were so many holes in him that they couldn't count. Everyone on the shipment was dead the ones that were not dead were shot again. After checking the bodies, they found out that two were women dressed up as men. The only two that were absent were, Jesse Bo-T and Mr. Diego, the boss.

When Jesse walked into Mr. Diego's office, he was packing, and he knew that he knew what had gone down.

He looked at Jesse and said, "Everyone, they killed everyone."

"I'm afraid so, Mr. Diego, we knew this was coming, we just didn't know when. There is one other thing Mr. Diego, there was another snitch we missed, but I found him." Jesse pulled out his .38 without the silencer. Diego looked at Jesse wide-eyed and said, "You? You Jesse? You are the informer!" "Me," Jesse said. He shot Diego three times, once in the heart, once between the eyes, and once in the head. He had to be sure.

****

Chapter 10

The federal building, sixth floor, room 623, Jesse walked in the office and told the secretary he had an appointment with agent Reebok. She asked him to wait and walked into Reebok's office, closed the door, came back in two minutes, and told him that he could go in.

Jesse walked in and was directed to one of the chairs in front of Reebok's desk, and they just looked at one another. "That was a decent job," Reebok said, "But the way we did it, I sure didn't like it. I also didn't like the deal we made, but I would have dealt with the devil to get those people. So, the deal was that you would turn over evidence, and turn the entire crew over to us for a clean slate. I'll tell you Mr. Bo-T, I think you should be in jail, if not dead with the rest of your crew. However, I will honor what I said, and since you already have the papers stating that you are to go free, I will stand by that. But you will tell me what I have always wanted to know; who killed Rosetta?"

"It was Basil," Jesse said. Of course, it wasn't, but how was he to know, Basil was dead.

"What about Eli?"

"Well, Luna killed Eli and Simon."

"Where is Simon's body?"

"I have no idea," Jesse said, "You see, Basil handled that, and he never mentioned where he buried the body. One of the other guys assisted him when he did that.

"And he is dead too," Reebok said, "Convenient!"

"No one told you to go in killing everyone. You could have saved a witness or something, but you didn't want to, did you Mr. Reebok? You were on a killing spree, and you got what you got."

"I thought you were an eyewitness, and you would tell us what we wanted to know."

"I told you everything. I honored my part of the deal, now I'm looking for you to do the same."

"I should put you behind bars right now Mr. Bo-T. To hell with that paperwork you are holding."

"Documents with your signature on it, and two witnesses I might add," Jesse said.

****

"You are back Jesse! How long are you staying this time?"

"I think until you throw me out Dottie, how about that?"

"Is there any chance of getting drawls around here?"

End

EPILOGUE

Two weeks, and he was out of there. That was a week longer than he could stay with any woman. He checked his finances and wondered where to go next. He thought of stopping at Paris or going on to Amsterdam. He had not been there for a while, but he had to stay away from Germany because they may remember him. The world is open to one who knows it, and there are many beautiful things in the world if you are open for it.

The ladies on the plane looked gorgeous, and he didn't know which one to grab first. He was like a kid in a candy store, and he liked what he saw, everything. He needed to see a doctor in Amsterdam because what he felt was not normal. However, when he is into sex, it feels damn right normal, and he felt like he would be doing it for a long time. Oh well, he may still see that doctor. Sex therapist, yeah, that's it, a sex therapist.

Damn the luck, halfway through the flight, some poor guy tried to pull a hijack. He guessed he should help stop him, but he was not headed for the pilot's area. He decided to leave it to the others, he was no hero, and he let the other passengers do the hero thing while he poured himself another drink. When he looked at the guy, the passengers had beat him up good. He guessed that the wannabe hijacker wished he would have stayed home.

There is always somebody messing up the deal, but on the other hand, the young lady sitting next to him was very frightened. She dropped her drink on her dress, grabbed him, and put her arms around him shaking. He felt obliged to consoler her. When the flight ended, they stopped at the airport hotel and stayed there for two days. She wanted to stay longer, but he was a one week, or two-day man. He caught another flight going in the opposite direction. He forgot where he was going, but it didn't matter, wherever he ended up was home.

End

ABOUT THE AUTHOR

Eddie J Martin

US AIR FORCE RETIRED

BOOKS BY THIS AUTHOR

Ruben's Bag

Ruben's Bad Side

Smooth... A Ruben Kane Novel

www.ingramcontent.com/pod-product-compliance
Lightning Source LLC
Chambersburg PA
CBHW071237170626
46809CB00008BA/3101